# Bella's Adventure

BY MICHÈLE DUFRESNE

PIONEER VALLEY EDUCATIONAL PRESS, INC.

# CONTENTS

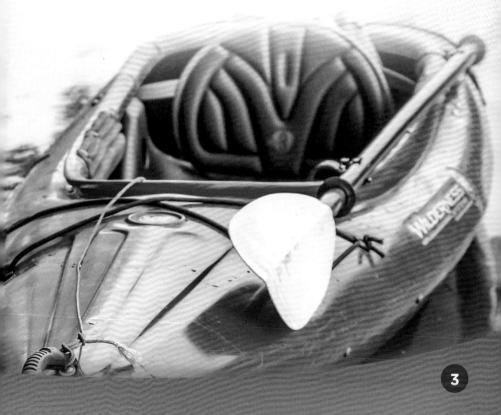

# Chapter 1: Where Is Bella?

Rosie woke up from a nap. She looked around. "Where is Bella?" she wondered. Bella wasn't on her pillow.

Rosie went outside. She walked around the yard. When the weather was nice, Bella sometimes liked to sleep in the dirt under a big, shady tree. But Bella wasn't outside.

Rosie went back in the house. She walked into the kitchen to look for Bella. Sometimes, Bella sat and waited for someone to drop something good on the floor. But Bella was not in the kitchen, either.

Rosie walked around the house. She looked in every room. Where was Bella? Finally, Rosie checked the porch. There was Bella, sleeping in a crate.

"Why is Bella in the crate?" thought Rosie.

Sometimes Mom and Dad put Bella in a crate to keep her out of trouble. Rosie was worried. Could Bella have gotten in trouble while Rosie was napping?

"Bella, wake up!" said Rosie. "Why are you in the crate. Were you a bad dog?"

Bella woke up. She stretched and yawned. "No," she said. "I am never a bad dog! Today I was an especially good dog."

Rosie was puzzled. Why would Bella be in the crate if she had been a good dog?

Rosie shook her head. "You must have gotten into some kind of trouble, Bella. I know Mom is getting the house ready for a dinner party. Did you eat something Mom was cooking?"

"No, I didn't eat anything," said Bella. "In fact, I'm starving!"

"Did you get on Mom's couch when you were dirty?" asked Rosie.

"No," Bella replied. "I did not get on Mom's couch when I was dirty. You need to believe me, Rosie. I have been a really good dog today!"

"OK, then why are you in the crate?" said Rosie.

"It's a long story," said Bella.

"That's OK," said Rosie. "I like a good, long story!"

# Chapter 2:
# A Porcupine in the Yard

Bella looked at Rosie. "When I tell you the story, you will see that I was a good dog. I do not deserve to be in the crate," Bella said. "But, I did have a bit of an adventure."

"Oh," said Rosie. "I can't wait to hear about your adventure!"

Rosie stretched out next to the crate to get comfortable. Bella often had interesting adventures. Rosie loved hearing about them.

"Did anything scary happen?" asked Rosie. "Did you get lost? Did you meet a big, scary animal?"

"No," said Bella. "You know that I never get lost. I did meet an animal, but it was not big or scary."

Rosie was glad there were no scary animals in the story. Scary animals made her anxious. Getting lost made her anxious, too. Rosie was glad Bella had not gotten lost.

"I will start at the beginning," said Bella.

"This adventure started with Jack," Bella began. "You know how Jack likes to pretend he is Super Dog?"

Rosie nodded. She knew how much Jack loved his Super Dog cape. Jack liked to pretend he could fly.

"Well, Jack was wearing his Super Dog cape today. He saw me and asked me to play Super Dog with him."

"Did you play with him?" asked Rosie.

"No way!" said Bella. "I was taking a nap on the porch. I told him to go away."

Rosie was not surprised. Jack often wanted someone to play Super Dog with him. But Bella and Rosie thought the game was silly.

"So, Jack went away. I settled back to sleep," said Bella. "I was having a nice dream about some yummy snacks. Then, suddenly, I smelled something."

Bella remembered how she had sniffed the air. She had looked around and seen a small, brown animal. It was near the edge of the woods. Bella had jumped up and run toward the little animal.

"When I got closer I saw it was a baby porcupine," said Bella. The baby porcupine saw Bella, and it began running as fast as it could into the woods. Bella followed the porcupine into the woods.

"Bella!" said Rosie. "Porcupines are dangerous! Even baby porcupines are dangerous. They have lots of sharp, pointy needles."

Bella nodded. "Yes, Rosie, that's true. But let me tell you what happened."

Bella told Rosie that Jack had started barking behind her. Bella stopped and turned around. She saw Jack following her into the woods. He was running along in his Super Dog cape.

Rosie was surprised to hear that Jack had followed Bella. Jack was scared of the woods. And he didn't like to leave home for any reason.

# Chapter 3:
# Sharp Pointed Needles

"Did you catch the baby porcupine?" asked Rosie. If Bella had caught a porcupine and brought it home, that would explain why she was in the crate.

"No," Bella said sadly. "I didn't catch the baby porcupine."

Rosie was glad Bella did not catch the baby porcupine. She was scared to think about what could have happened if Bella had caught a baby porcupine.

"So what happened?" asked Rosie.

Bella told Rosie how she went into the woods and looked around. She couldn't see the porcupine anywhere. She sniffed the grass and bushes. She tried to figure out where the porcupine had gone.

"Was Jack still following you?" asked Rosie.

"Yes!" said Bella.

Rosie was puzzled to learn that Jack had followed Bella into the woods. Did he think he could help catch the porcupine? Maybe he felt brave enough to go in the woods because he was wearing his Super Dog cape.

Bella continued telling her story. "Help me find the porcupine," Bella had said to Jack. So Jack started to sniff around.

"I followed the scent of the porcupine deeper into the woods," Bella told Rosie.

"The woods can be scary!" said Rosie. Rosie never went into the woods by herself.

"The woods are not scary to me," Bella said proudly.

Bella loved the woods. She loved wandering around smelling things. Bella could stay in the woods all day. She loved chasing after squirrels and rabbits and toads.

"So—did you find the baby porcupine?" asked Rosie.

"Yes," said Bella. "You know that I am very good at tracking things. Jack and I followed the scent to a hollow log that was lying across the path. We saw the baby porcupine trying to climb into the log," said Bella.

Rosie was confused. "What? You told me you didn't get the porcupine!" she said.

"No," said Bella. "I didn't get it. I guess you could say it this way: The porcupine got me."

"Oh, no!" said Rosie.

Bella was about to nip the porcupine when it turned and ran toward her. All of a sudden, Bella had twenty needles sticking into her nose and ears! Bella told Rosie all about the sharp, pointy needles.

"Oh, dear!" said Rosie. "What did you do then?"

"Well, I backed up right away," said Bella. "Jack started barking like crazy. He was running around in circles."

"Did any of the quills get Jack?" Rosie asked.

"No," said Bella. "Jack barked a lot. He acted like the quills had hurt him, but all the quills went into me!"

"They really hurt," continued Bella, "so I rubbed my nose in the dirt to try to get them to come out."

When Bella rubbed her face in the mud, it made the needles stick more deeply into her nose and ears. So, Bella raced toward the nearby river. She couldn't stand the pain from the porcupine's sharp quills! All she wanted to do was to jump in the cool water.

Jack tried to follow, but he couldn't run as fast as Bella. Jack could never run as fast as Bella. On this day, Bella was running extra fast because of the pain from the porcupine's sharp quills.

When Bella reached the river, she turned and looked for Jack. Jack was not behind her. She could hear him barking, somewhere in the woods.

"I ran to the river and jumped right in," Bella told Rosie.

"Did that help?" Rosie asked.

"A little bit," said Bella. "The quills didn't come out, but the water felt cool so they didn't hurt as much."

"Then, I smelled something!" said Bella. "Something good!"

"Did the smell have anything to do with you being a good dog?" asked Rosie. "I am wondering what you did that was so good."

"I told you it was a long story," said Bella. "You have to wait for the part where I am good. But," Bella added, "you can already see that I was not bad."

Rosie wasn't sure about that. She thought Mom would not like the part about the baby porcupine and the sharp quills. She thought Dad would be upset that Bella let Jack follow her into the woods.

But Rosie did not mention this to Bella. "What was the smell?" she asked.

# Chapter 4:
# A Good Smell

Bella remembered climbing out of the nice cool river and sniffing the air. She quickly forgot about the quills sticking in her nose! She smelled something good to eat, and that made her forget all about the pain.

Bella looked around, trying to figure out where the good smell was coming from. She noticed that a boat was pulled up onto the shore. Bella trotted over to the boat and sniffed. A wonderful smell was coming from inside the boat.

Bella looked over the edge of the boat. She saw that someone had left a sandwich sitting there. It was not just a crumb, either. Most of a whole sandwich was in the boat!

"It was a turkey sandwich," Bella told Rosie. "Someone just left a turkey sandwich in the boat— probably for a hungry dog like me!"

"Hmmm," Rosie thought to herself. "Maybe."

"So I jumped into the boat," said Bella. "I gobbled up the turkey sandwich! I was hungry after all that tracking and getting quills in my nose and ears. That sandwich was delicious!"

After Bella ate the sandwich, she felt sleepy. Bella told Rosie there had also been a comfortable mat in the boat, so she decided to take a nap. Bella had curled up on the mat and gone to sleep.

"What about Jack?" Rosie asked. "Did you forget about Jack?"

"I didn't forget him," said Bella. "I just thought Jack had walked home. Or I thought maybe he was walking slowly. I thought he would catch up to me."

"Oh," Rosie said. She was getting worried about Jack. Did he ever make it home? Rosie hadn't seen Jack for a while. She was scared for Jack. Maybe he was still in the woods somewhere.

"Did you ever find Jack?" asked Rosie. "Is he OK? Did you lose Jack? Is that why you are in the crate?"

"Wait, Rosie!" Bella said. "Let me finish my story."

# Chapter 5: A Nap for Bella

"All right," said Rosie. "You went to sleep on the boat. What happened after that?"

"Oh, I was having such a nice nap," said Bella. "I was dreaming about giant turkey sandwiches. They were floating on the water."

"I think sandwiches would sink in the water," Rosie said.

"It was a dream!" said Bella. "And in my dream, the sandwiches were floating!"

Rosie smiled. Bella had crazy dreams.

"Then what happened?" Rosie asked.

Bella remembered that she had heard Jack barking. He sounded very anxious.

Bella stood up and looked over the edge of the boat.

"I looked out from the boat," Bella told Rosie, "but it wasn't on the shore anymore. The boat was floating down the river!"

"Oh, dear!" said Rosie.

"I could see Jack from the boat. He was standing near the edge of the river. It was Jack's crying that woke me up," said Bella.

"Poor Jack," Rosie said. She could picture Jack crying by the river. If he was far away from home and couldn't find Bella, he must have been very scared.

Rosie knew how scared she would be if she was in the woods and couldn't find Bella. "What did you do next?" Rosie asked.

"I called out to Jack," said Bella. "When he saw me in the boat, he looked up and ran to the water's edge."

Rosie thought Jack must have been very happy to see Bella. But what could he do? Bella was in the boat floating down the river. The river was dangerous. It was much too big to swim across.

Rosie shivered at the thought of the big, wide river. She knew Bella had made it home, because now

Bella was safe and sound in the crate. But it was very scary to think about Bella floating down a huge river in a boat all by herself!

"I told Jack to run and get help," said Bella. "But Jack just cried and cried as he watched me float down the river."

"Oh, dear," said Rosie.

"But I had an idea. I told him that he was Super Dog. Super Dog needed to run and get help. "

"You helped me find the porcupine," Bella told Jack. "Now Super Dog can help find Mom or Dad!"

# Chapter 6:
# The Boat Ride

Soon Bella lost sight of Jack. The current was moving the boat faster and faster down the river. Bella didn't know whether Jack had headed back home. Maybe he was still crying in the same place near the shore.

When the boat moved past houses on the shore, Bella began to bark. Bella said she barked because she hoped that if people in the houses noticed, they would come to the river to help her.

"Did anyone hear you barking?" asked Rosie.

"No," said Bella. "I guess my barking was not loud enough. No one came out of any of the houses. I thought I might jump out of the boat. I could try to swim. But I thought if I was not in the boat, I might get carried away in the current."

"Oh, no!" said Rosie shivering with fright. "Were you afraid?"

"I wasn't afraid," said Bella. "I thought someone would find me eventually. I was worried I might miss dinner, though. I was starving!"

Rosie knew that if she had been in the boat with Bella, she would not have been thinking about dinner! "What happened next?" she asked.

Bella continued telling the story of her adventure.

She told Rosie that the boat floated around a curve in the river where trees had fallen into the water. The boat stopped moving when it hit some branches. When the boat stopped moving, Bella jumped out onto the branches.

"Thank goodness for the trees!" Rosie cried. "You were a brave dog to jump out of the boat, Bella," she said.

"Yes, Rosie, you can see that I was a good dog," said Bella. "But listen to what happened next, and you will learn why I am a very good dog."

# Chapter 7:
# The Search for Bella

"What else could possibly happen?" asked Rosie. "Didn't you run right home?"

"I couldn't!" said Bella. "I wanted to come home, but my foot got stuck between two branches. I pulled and pulled, but I couldn't get it free."

"Oh, dear!" said Rosie.

Later, Bella learned that Mom and Dad had realized Bella and Jack were both missing. Mom had walked up the driveway to talk to the neighbors. Dad headed into the woods to search for the dogs.

The neighbors said they had not seen Bella or Jack. But when Dad went into the woods, he heard Jack crying.

"Good for Jack!" said Rosie. "Good for Super Dog!"

Bella nodded. "Dad followed the sounds of Jack crying. He found Jack waiting by the river," said Bella. "When he saw Dad, Jack ran along the river sniffing and looking for me. Dad ran along the river following Jack."

"Then Dad found you and brought you home," said Rosie. Rosie enjoyed the story of Bella's adventure. "Dad put you in the crate when you got home. You are a good dog because you taught Jack how to sniff!"

"No," said Bella. "That is not the end of the story. Listen! I did something really, really good."

"This is such an exciting adventure," said Rosie. "What happened next?"

Bella told Rosie that she saw Dad and Jack coming along a path near the river. Jack spotted Bella first, and he started barking like crazy.

Bella said Dad climbed out onto the logs. He picked her up and carried her to shore. Dad tucked Bella under one arm. Then he leaned over to pick up Jack and put him under his other arm. Dad said, "Oh, Bella! What kind of trouble have you gotten yourself into?"

"Was Dad mad?" asked Rosie. "It's a good thing you don't weigh very much!"

"Dad started down the path," said Bella. "He was carrying me under one arm and Jack under the other. He was huffing and puffing a little because it was hot."

"I started to squirm," Bella said. "I wanted to get down and walk home by myself. Dad told me to stop wiggling. He said I wasn't going to get a chance to run away again."

"Oh dear," said Rosie. "He thought you ran away?"

"Yes!" said Bella. "Can you believe that? I was minding my own business. I was quietly sleeping in a nice shady spot. Then I smelled a porcupine in our yard! What was I supposed to do?"

"You are right, it was all the porcupine's fault," Rosie laughed. "But Bella, you know if you hadn't gone in the boat to get that sandwich, you would not have ended up in the river."

"That was not my fault!" said Bella.

"Whatever you say, Bella," said Rosie. "So then what happened? Did Dad carry you home and put you in the crate?"

# Chapter 8:
# In the Mud

"Hold on, I'm getting to that part," said Bella. "I really wanted to get down. So I wiggled some more. There were muddy spots along the path. Then Dad slipped while I was wiggling."

"Uh, oh," said Rosie.

"Dad fell into the mud," said Bella. "We all ended up in the mud."

"You, Jack, and Dad?" cried Rosie. "All of you landed in the mud?"

"Yes," said Bella. "The mud felt so nice and cool! I was really hot, so I rolled around in it for a while."

"I see," said Rosie. "Now I think I understand why you are in the crate."

"Wait, listen!" said Bella. "I am getting to the best part of the story."

Bella told Rosie that Jack had started whining about his cape getting dirty from the mud. Dad had muttered a few bad words. Then Dad stopped walking.

"That's when I realized that Dad did not know how to get home!" Bella said. "He used the belt from his pants to make a leash for me, and I led Dad and Jack out of the woods." Bella told Rosie proudly.

"Really?" Rosie asked. "You think Dad needed you to help him find the way home?"

"Yes!" said Bella. "Dad made a leash for me, and I led everyone home!"

"Oh, hmmm," said Rosie.

"When we got there, Mom was mad because I was muddy," said Bella. "And she was upset about the quills, even though they were really small. Mom had to take me to the vet to have them removed."

"Oh, dear," said Rosie.

"Then Mom gave me a bath," Bella said sadly. "And she told me to get in the crate."

Bella looked at Rosie. "It was so unfair! I was a good dog the whole day," she said. "You can see that, right?"

"Of course," Rosie said. "You're a really good dog, Bella. And that was quite an exciting adventure."

"It was a great adventure!" said Bella. "Too bad you missed the whole thing."

Rosie nodded her head and smiled. "Yes, that's too bad," she said.